A SPECIAL GUEST has been invited –
Have you put the tinsel on the tree?
When he arrives you'll be delighted –
Is your stocking up for him to see?
I've never been quite so excited –

I hope he's got a present
just for **me!**

For Iggy and Bo – M.L.

To my mum, dad and brothers,
Matt and Curtis; thank you for the love,
support and mince pies. – S.C.

EGMONT

First published in Great Britain in 2020 by
Egmont Books

An imprint of HarperCollins*Publishers*
1 London Bridge Street
London SE1 9GF

www.egmontbooks.co.uk

Text and illustrations copyright © Matt Lucas 2020
Illustrations by Scott Coello.

Matt Lucas has asserted his moral rights.

ISBN 978 0 7555 0180 9
Printed in Great Britain.
71490/001

A CIP catalogue record for this title is available from the British Library.

Stay safe online. Egmont is not responsible for content hosted by third parties.

Egmont takes its responsibility to the planet and its inhabitants very seriously.
We aim to use papers from well-managed forests run by responsible suppliers.

Adult supervision is advised for some of the activities within the book.
Always ask an adult for help when using glue, paint and scissors.
Wear protective clothing and cover surfaces to avoid staining.

MERRY CHRISTMAS, BAKED POTATO

MATT LUCAS

ILLUSTRATED BY
SCOTT COELLO

EGMONT

If you look high up in the sky
(I'm talking higher than a parrot)

You'll see a root
veg flying by
(and no I do not
mean a carrot)

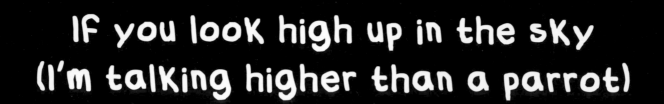

We've spent
the whole year
waiting for
this day . . .

It is really quite a sight
to see a spud so busy –
Two billion houses in one night
He must be getting dizzy!

I've picked
a yak up

in case the reindeer
need to take a break . . .

Oh Santa Baked Potato, we love you!

Who knows what gifts he'll bring?

A tricycle

a trumpet

or a train set?

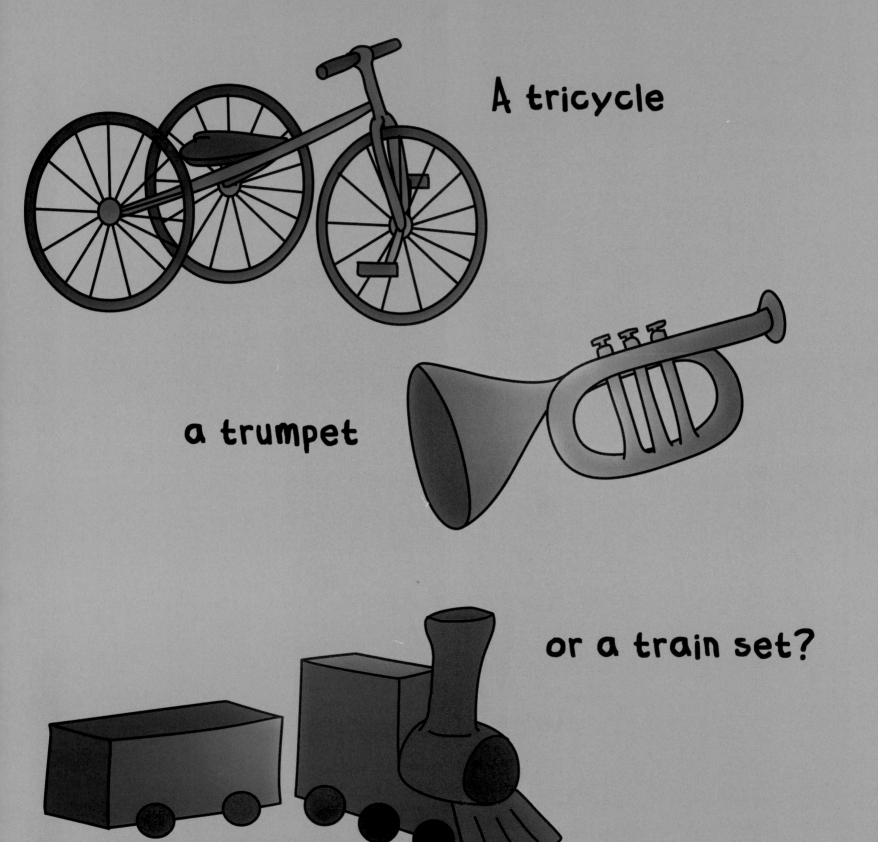

A purple
dressing gown

a teddy bear

a snorkel and some flippers?

A funny puppet clown with wavy hair to entertain the nippers

A super soaker that you'll love to spray . . . .

SANTA BAKED POTATO'S ON HIS WAY!

What a Kerfuffle! The reindeer went the wrong direction . . .

I'M SURE WE'VE BEEN TWICE TO THIS TOWN

Oh Santa Baked Potato,

ENJOY YOURSELF WITH THESE FESTIVE ACTIVITIES!

KINDNESS CARDS

Spread kindness this Christmas! Make and decorate your own special cards – write a kind message or suggest a kind, helpful or fun activity inside each one. For example, 'I love you' or 'Collect a hug' or 'I promise I'll tidy up'. Hide the cards around the house and wait till your family find them. You could sign the cards with your name – or give yourself a secret elf name!

SILLY CHRISTMAS KARAOKE

Write down your favourite Christmas songs on pieces of paper, fold them up and put them in a bowl (or hat). Next write down some silly costumes that you can create at home (for example, Santa, a princess or a pirate) and put them in another bowl. Now ask each person in your family to pick a piece of paper from each bowl – and perform their Christmas song in costume. Don't forget to use silly voices!

POTATO ELF PRINTS

Ask an adult to slice a raw potato in half lengthways. Use the potato and some poster paint to make prints on a piece of paper or card. Once the prints are dry, decorate them with funny faces and elf outfits. Why not give your potato elves names too?

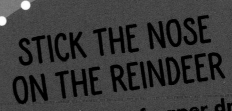

STICK THE NOSE ON THE REINDEER

On a large piece of paper draw a reindeer – all except the nose – and stick in onto a wall or pinboard. On a separate piece of paper, draw and colour a big red nose. Cut it out with the help of a grown-up and put some Blu Tack on the back. Now take it in turns to wear a blindfold and try to stick the nose onto the reindeer! Who will get the closest?

BAKED POTATO PUPPET

With an adult's help, cut out a potato shape from some card, making it about as big as your hand. Make two small holes in the bottom and poke your fingers through. Colour your puppet and decorate it with eyes and a big potato smile. You could even add a Santa suit and hat. Hey presto – your very own Baked Potato pal!

MATT LUCAS is an actor, writer and comedian, first coming to prominence in *Shooting Stars* with Vic Reeves and Bob Mortimer. Together with David Walliams, he reaped massive success with the smash-hit series *Little Britain*. The three BBC series and two Christmas specials won nearly every award for which they were nominated, including three BAFTAs, three NTAs and two International Emmy Awards.

Matt's film roles have included *Alice in Wonderland*, *Bridesmaids*, *Paddington*, *Missing Link* and *Gnomeo & Juliet*. He has appeared the US comedy series *Community*, *Portlandia* and *Fresh Off the Boat*, while back in the UK, he starred as series regular Nardole in *Doctor Who*, as well as fulfilling a lifetime ambition to appear in *Les Misérables*, playing Thénardier. Matt regularly presents shows on BBC Radio 2 and is the new co-host of *The Great British Bake Off*.

In spring 2020, Matt wrote and recorded a brand-new version of his song *Thank You, Baked Potato* to raise money for FeedNHS. It went to the top of the download charts and Matt has since performed the song with a host of celebrities, including Brian May, Gary Barlow and the cast of *Coronation Street*. The picture book version, also raising money for FeedNHS, was an Amazon chart-topper.

SCOTT COELLO creates animations and illustrations under the alias Cribble. Cribble's humorous artwork and short films, from stories of human struggle to vignettes about dog farts, have been viewed by millions worldwide. *Merry Christmas, Baked Potato* is Cribble's second picture book for children.